IF YOU EVER MEET A WHALE

Poems selected by Myra Cohn Livingston

Illustrated by Leonard Everett Fisher

Holiday House / New York

To Thomas and Timothy

M.C.L.

To Samuel Benjamin

L.E.F

Text copyright © 1992 by Myra Cohn Livingston
Illustrations copyright © 1992 by Leonard Everett Fisher
Printed in the United States of America
All rights reserved
First Edition

Library of Congress Cataloging-in-Publication Data
If You Ever Meet a Whale/selected by Myra Cohn Livingston; illustrated by
Leonard Everett Fisher.
p.   cm.
Summary: A collection of poems about whales, by such authors as
Jane Yolen, Theodore Roethke, and John Ciardi.
ISBN 0-8234-0940-6
1. Whales—Juvenile poetry.   2. Children's poetry, American.
[1. Whales—Poetry.   2. American poetry—Collections.]
I. Livingston, Myra Cohn.   II. Fisher, Leonard Everett, ill.
PS595.W395S6   1992   91-36265   CIP   AC
811.008′036—dc20

CONTENTS

Why Noah Praised the Whale

The elephants on Noah's Ark
  Ate seven bales of hay
For forty days and forty nights
  —Seven whole bales a day!

Two hundred eighty times in all
  As he pitched another bale
The animals heard Noah cry,
  Thank Heaven for the whale!

"I like my elephants, of course,
  But once our trip is done,
They will be fat on Ararat
  And I'll be skin and bone

"From pitching hay day after day,
  Bale after dusty bale.
And that is why I often cry,
  Thank Heaven for the whale!

"It's bigger than the elephant
  But wise creation gave it
A safe snug sea, and that saves me
  The bother of having to save it.

"It saves itself. With elephants
  I have to do the saving.
And that's a thought I think a lot
  when I am down here slaving

"To pitch them hay day after day,
  Bale after dusty bale.
And that is why I often cry
  Thank Heaven for the whale!"

JOHN CIARDI

5

The Constant Whales

In the lagoon, in the lagoon,
the whales spoon, the whales spawn,
and spume and spume,
       and the ocean rolls and the ocean rolls.

Behemoths from the Bering Sea
marking their places with flames of spume,
thousands of miles to the great lagoon, in Baja,
       and the ocean rolls and the ocean rolls.

Forever and ever, ever and ever,
the whales have swum to the great lagoon,
though the world grows old and turns and turns,
       and the ocean rolls and rolls.

FELICE HOLMAN

8

Jack Was Every Inch a Sailor

Now, 'twas twenty-five or thirty years since Jack first saw the light;
He came into this world of woe one dark and stormy night.
He was born on board his father's ship as she was lying to
'Bout twenty-five or thirty miles south-east of Bacalhao.

CHORUS

Jack was ev'ry inch a sailor,
Five and twenty years a whaler;
Jack was ev'ry inch a sailor,
He was born upon the bright blue sea.

When Jack grew up to be a man, he went to Labrador;
He fished in Indian Harbour where his father fished before;
On his returning in the fog, he met a heavy gale,
And Jack was swept into the sea and swallowed by a whale.

The whale went straight for Baffin's Bay 'bout ninety knots an hour,
And ev'rytime he'd blow a spray, he'd send it in a shower.
"Oh, now," says Jack unto himself, "I must see what he's about."
He caught the whale all by the tail and turned him inside out.

Anonymous

The Whale

There was a most Monstrous Whale:
He had no Skin, he had no Tail.
When he tried to Spout, that Great Big Lubber,
The best he could do was Jiggle his Blubber.

THEODORE ROETHKE

The Whales Off Wales

With walloping tails, the whales off Wales
Whack waves to wicked whitecaps.
And while they snore on their watery floor,
They wear wet woolen nightcaps.

The whales! the whales! the whales off Wales,
They're always spouting fountains.
And as they glide through the tilting tide,
They move like melting mountains.

X.J. KENNEDY

Blue

Fifty tons of muscle
seventy tons of skin & blood & bone
your tongue bigger than an elephant
your glad heart six men could carry
your enormous stone-still eye

& this song half way to China
from you, Blue, fat with she-calf
graceful as a cloud sailing down
the long night of the sea

13

If You Ever

If you ever ever ever ever ever,
    If you ever ever ever meet a whale,
You must never never never never never,
    You must never never never touch its tail:
For if you ever ever ever ever ever,
    If you ever ever ever touch its tail,
You will never never never never never,
    You will never never meet another whale.

ANONYMOUS

The Song of the Mother Whale

Side by side,
side by side
mother and baby
glide
soft and warm
under the greenblue
under the bluegreen sea.

Mother whale,
big as Ohio,
sings this song
to her tiny duaghter:
What is that
shadow over our heads?

Dive down,
dive down
deep in the water!
It's a ship
Those are humans
floating above us!
They may mean us harm!

Men with harpoons
and sailors with
spears
have often pursued us—
some want to eat us,
some want to sell us,
all want to use us!

Stay close to me, darling
close by my side,
We'll hide
under blue mountains,
we'll swim
through gray valleys
five miles below us—

and no one
will find us
and no one
will touch us
and only the
friendly dolphins
will know us.

Safe and free,
safe and free,
let's swim
side by side
under the greenblue
under the greenblue
under the bluegreen sea.

RUTH WHITMAN

Whale

The whale can swallow
a thousand sardines;
he is the biggest
of fish soup tureens.

N.M. BODECKER

Sea Canary

The white whale or beluga was called the sea canary
by 18th-century English whalers, for its chirps and
whistles and moans could be heard above the water.

We heard her, white and weary,
singing a last song,
her whistle following us
into the night.
Did she sing of her young
still brown behind her?
Or of the bottoms of waves
made light by the moon?
Or did she sing of her death,
the harps still heavy in her bones,
pulling her toward the air
and the long dark shanks of our hold.

JANE YOLEN

21

My Eyes Are Tired

My eyes are tired,
my worn-out eyes,
which never more will follow the narwhal
when shooting up from the deep,
in order to break the waves of the sea,
and my muscles will nevermore tremble
when I seize the harpoon,
ijaja—a—ijaja—aje.

Wish that the souls
of the great sea animals I killed
would help me to get
my heavy thoughts to a distance.
Wish that the memory
of all my great hunts
might lift me out of the weakness of old age,
ijaja—a—ijaja—aje.

Let my breath blow a song
Of all this which calls to mind
my youth.
My song breaks from my throat
with the breath of my life.

GREENLAND ESKIMO

Prayer to the Whale

Whale, I want you to come near me so that I will get hold of your
heart and deceive it, so that I will have strong legs
and not be trembling and excited when the whale
comes and I spear him.

Whale, you must not run out to sea when I spear you.

Whale, if I spear you, I want my spear to spike your heart.

Harpoon, when I use you, I want you to go to the heart.

Whale, when I spear at you and miss you, I want you to take
hold of my spear with your hands.

Whale, do not break my canoe, for I am going to do good to
you. I am going to put eagle-down and cedar-bark on your back.

Whale, if I use only one canoe to kill you, I want to kill you
dead.

NOOTKA INDIAN

25

Whale at Twilight

The sea is enormous, but calm with evening and sunset,
rearranging its islands for the night, changing its ocean
   blues,
smoothing itself against the reefs, without playfulness,
   without thought.
No stars are out, only sea birds flying to distant reefs.
No vessels intrude, no lobstermen haul their pots,
only somewhere out toward the horizon a thin column of
   water appears
and disappears again, and then rises once more,
tranquil as a fountain in a garden where no wind blows.

ELIZABETH COATSWORTH

Watching Gray Whales

Their skin is gray-green.
They look like copper
    that is corroded.
Barnacles on them
    look like sharp
    rocks that are
    fixed to the
    sliding wall
    of a building
    under water.
They are of
    a different
    world, slow,
    watching you
    while you
    watch them.
They are patient.
They survive.

J.S. BAIRD

27

Stranding

What pushes me
toward the shallows
making my body
a burden?
What is this confusion?
Why can't I bear left
and follow the one
star
      that leads
to the great depth
and a lightness
of being, a joy?
What is this pain
in my head
this pain,
beating like a storm,
that has followed me
since I passed by
      that metal ship?

EMANUEL DI PASQUALE

29

Beached

This beautiful barnacled bulk
is beached now,
No more to glide through
secret gardens of the sea;
No more to breach the glassy calm,
then plunge down in plumes of blue.
Soon it will be bare bleached bones.
The bones will be beautiful too.

TONY JOHNSTON

The Whale Ghost

When we've emptied
the sea of the
last great
whale

will he come
rising
from a deep remembered
dive

sending from his
blowhole
a ghostly fog
of spout?

Will he call
with haunting cry

to his herd that
rode the
seas with joyous
ease,

to the whale that swam
beside him,

to the calf?

Will we hear his
sad song
echoing
over the water?

LILIAN MOORE

31

ACKNOWLEDGMENTS

Grateful acknowledgment is made to the following poets, whose work was especially commissioned for this book:

John Baird for "Watching Gray Whales." Copyright © 1992 by John Baird.

Emanuel di Pasquale for "Stranding." Copyright © 1992 by Emanuel di Pasquale.

Tony Johnston for "Beached." Copyright © 1992 by Tony Johnston.

J. Patrick Lewis for "Blue." Copyright © 1992 by J. Patrick Lewis.

Ruth Whitman for "The Song of the Mother Whale." Copyright © 1992 by Ruth Whitman.

Grateful acknowledgment is made for the following reprints:

Curtis Brown Ltd. for "The Whales Off Wales" from *One Winter Night in August* by X.J. Kennedy. Copyright © 1975 by X.J. Kennedy; for "Sea Canary" by Jane Yolen. Copyright © 1990 by Jane Yolen.

Doubleday for "The Whale" from *The Collected Poems of Theodore Roethke* by Theodore Roethke. Copyright © 1961. Used by permission of Doubleday, a division of Bantam, Doubleday, Dell Publishing Group, Inc.

Houghton Mifflin Co. for "Why Noah Praised the Whale" from *Fast and Slow* by John Ciardi. Copyright © 1975 by John Ciardi. Reprinted by permission of Houghton Mifflin Co.

James Houston for "My Eyes Are Tired" from *Songs of the Dream People*, edited by James Houston. Copyright © 1972 by James Houston.

Macmillan Publishing Company for "Whale" from *Snowman Sniffles and Other Verse* by N.M. Bodecker. Reprinted with permission of Margaret K. McElderry Books, an imprint of Macmillan Publishing Company. Copyright © 1983 by N.M. Bodecker; for "Whale at Twilight" from *Down Half the World* by Elizabeth Coatsworth. Reprinted with permission of Macmillan Publishing Company. Copyright © 1950 and renewed 1978 by Elizabeth Coatsworth Beston. Originally appeared in *The New Yorker*; for "The Constant Whales" from *The Song in My Head* by Felice Holman. Reprinted with permission of Charles Scribner's Sons, an imprint of Macmillan Publishing Company. Copyright © 1985 by Felice Holman; for "The Whale Ghost" from *Something New Begins* by Lilian Moore. Reprinted with permission of Atheneum Publishers, an imprint of Macmillan Publishing Company. Copyright © 1982 by Lilian Moore.